Randall

Emma's Pet

Emma's Pet

by David McPhail

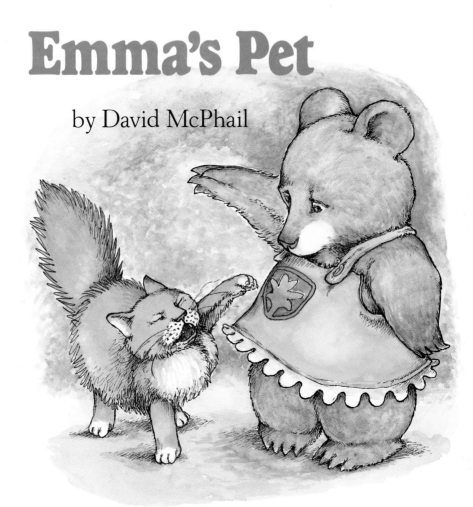

E. P. Dutton   New York

for Ashly Lee LaBrie

Copyright © 1985 by David McPhail
All rights reserved.
Unicorn is a registered trademark of E. P. Dutton.
Library of Congress number 85-4414
ISBN 0-525-44430-0
Published in the United States by E. P. Dutton,
2 Park Avenue, New York, N.Y. 10016,
a division of NAL Penguin Inc.
Published simultaneously in Canada by
Fitzhenry & Whiteside Limited, Toronto
Editor: Ann Durell   Designer: Isabel Warren-Lynch
Printed in Hong Kong by South China Printing Co.
First Unicorn Edition 1988   COBE
10 9 8 7 6 5 4 3 2 1

"I want a pet," Emma told her mother one day.
"You have a pet," said her mother.

"Fluffy's not cuddly," said Emma.
"I want a big soft cuddly pet."

So Emma went looking for a pet.

The first thing she found was a bug.
Even Emma couldn't say that was cuddly.

The mouse she found was soft and cuddly,
but it wasn't big.

The bird had nice soft feathers…

but it was too busy

feeding its family to be anybody's pet.

The frog wasn't soft and cuddly,
but it might have made a good pet...

if it hadn't taken a bath with Emma's mother.

The snake she picked up was *too* cuddly for Emma.

Then she got a fish…

but that was too wet and slippery.

And the dog she brought home
already belonged to someone else.

Emma was sad.

She sat down on a rock and began to cry.

The rock moved.
It was a turtle!

But it wasn't any softer or any more cuddly than a rock.

And then Emma saw the biggest, softest,
cuddliest thing she had ever seen.

It was her father!

"Will you be my pet?" she asked.

"Always," said her father. "Will you be mine?"
"Yes," said Emma.

And she hugged her new big soft cuddly pet.
And it hugged her right back.